TESSA KRAILING

The Petsitters Club

7. Oscar the Fancy Rat

Illustrated by Jan Lewis

BARRON'S

First edition for the United States, Canada, and the Philippine Republic published by Barron's Educational Series, Inc., 1999.

First published in Great Britain in 1998 by Scholastic Children's Books, Commonsealth House, 1-19 New Oxford Street, London WC1A 1NU, UK

Barron's Educational Series, Inc.
250 Wireless Boulevard
Hauppauge, New York 11788
http://www.barronseduc.com

ISBN 0-7641-0692-9
Library of Congress Catalog Card No. 98-31032

Printed in the United States of America
9 8 7 6 5 4 3 2

Chapter 1

Alice

Every Saturday morning the Petsitters met in Sam's kitchen to discuss what had happened during the previous week— and on this particular Saturday they all had gloomy faces.

"Nobody's asked me to do any new jobs for ages," Sam reported. "How about you?"

Matthew and Jovan both shook their heads.

Suddenly Sam realized there was one Petsitter missing. "Where's Katie?" she asked.

"She's coming later," said Matthew, Katie's older brother. "But I don't think anyone's asked her to petsit their creepy-crawlies either."

"Perhaps nobody's seen our sign," said Jovan, "Perhaps it's been taken down by mistake?"

Sam shook her head. "No, it's still there. I saw it yesterday."

Their sign hung on the supermarket bulletin board. It said:

TOO BUSY TO FEED YOUR CAT?
TOO ~~OLD~~ TIRED TO WALK YOUR DOG?
CALL 555-8934 FOR YOUR LOCAL
PETSITTING SERVICE

ANY PET LOOKED AFTER
LARGE OR SMALL
WE ARE THE EXPERTS!

"It's a good thing Matthew's still got his regular job," said Jovan. "Walking his neighbor's dog."

Matthew sighed. "To tell the truth, I'm a bit fed up with it. Every morning and evening I walk Bruno up to the park and

5

back again. It gets pretty boring after a while. I'd rather do a paper route."

"You wouldn't get any community service points for a paper route," Sam pointed out. "And if we want to win that Cup we're going to need all the points we can get."

The Community Service Cup was awarded each term by their principal, Mr. Grantham. To win it they had to do jobs for people, but instead of money they got points, provided the person they'd helped signed a special form. Then, whichever group of children had earned the most points would win the Cup.

Jovan nodded. "We're still in second place and there's only a week to go."

Sam groaned. "We've just got to get some more jobs!"

At that moment the door opened and Katie walked in, followed by a cage on legs. At least, that's what it looked like. A large cage with a pair of legs clad in white socks and red shoes.

"This is my friend Alice Hope," said Katie. "She wants us to look after her rat."

"Her *rat*!" echoed the other three Petsitters.

Katie turned to the cage on legs. "Put Oscar on the table, Alice."

Once the cage was lifted onto the table, they could see that Alice Hope was a small girl with anxious brown eyes and brown hair with bangs.

"Oscar was a birthday present from her uncle," Katie explained. "Trouble is, her mom doesn't like rats."

"A lot of people don't like rats," said Jovan, eyeing the cage with mistrust. "They're dirty and spread diseases."

Two large tears appeared in Alice's eyes. Her mouth began to tremble.

"You're thinking of wild rats," Katie said quickly. "Oscar's what they call a fancy rat. Take him out, Alice, and show them how tame he is."

Alice blinked hard. She unfastened the door of the cage and reached inside for a small white animal, half hidden among the wood shavings. Carefully she set him down on the table, where he sat making little sniffling movements with his nose.

"He's got pink eyes," said Matthew.

"And a very long tail," said Jovan.

"And whiskers." Sam held out her finger for Oscar to sniff at. "What does he eat?"

"Mainly hamster food," said Katie. "But his favorite is hard-boiled eggs."

"Ugh!" Sam grimaced. If there was one thing she hated it was hard-boiled eggs!

"Her mom says she's got to get rid of him," Katie explained. "But Alice doesn't want to. So I said we'd look after him for her."

"For how long?!" asked Sam. "I mean, we can't look after him forever."

"Not forever," said Katie. "Only until her mom changes her mind."

"What if she doesn't?!" asked Matthew.

The tears came back into Alice's eyes. Her mouth began to tremble again.

Sam said hastily, "Oh, well . . . I suppose we could look after him for a little while. We can't really afford to turn down any job just now. As long as Alice signs the form so we get our points . . ."

"She'll sign it," said Katie. "I've already told her about the Cup."

Matthew stared hard at Alice. "She doesn't say much, does she?"

"She's shy," Katie explained.

"The question is," said Sam, "which one of us is going to look after Oscar?"

"Not me," said Jovan quickly. "My dad says he's got enough animals to look after in his veterinary office without having any extra at home."

"Not me, either," said Matthew. "I've got enough to do, walking Mrs. Wimpole's dog twice a day. I think Katie should be the one to look after him. After all, she's Alice's friend."

Katie shook her head. "I only do creepy-crawlies."

They all turned to look at Sam, including Alice, with her anxious brown eyes.

"Oh, all right," said Sam at last. "He can stay here. I don't suppose my dad will mind."

But she was wrong. Later that day, when she carried the cage into her father's den, he wouldn't even look at Oscar.

"Ugh!" he said with a shudder. "I can't stand rats. Take it away."

"But he's a very nice little rat," said Sam, surprised. "If you'd only look at him I'm sure you'd like him."

"And I'm sure I wouldn't! Sorry, Sam, but if there's one animal I won't have in the house, it's a rat."

Chapter 2

Little Rascal

When Matthew told the others that walking Bruno every day was a boring job, he hadn't exactly been telling the truth. The truth was that sometimes it was boring, but at other times it could be pretty exciting. A bit *too* exciting, to be honest.

Because Bruno was a digger.

17

If he found a rabbit hole, he would dive down it headfirst and disappear for ages. And if there wasn't a hole handy, he would dig one. The last time, the groundskeeper at the park had told Matthew he'd better keep that dog of his under control, or else. Matthew had tried to explain that Bruno wasn't his dog, but the groundskeeper was too angry to listen.

On Sunday morning he took Bruno into the park as usual. Bruno pulled at the leash, obviously wanting his freedom. After a while Matthew's arm began to ache. "Well, if I let you off," he said sternly, "will you promise not to dig any holes?"

Bruno wagged his tail. Matthew bent down to unclip the leash and Bruno trotted off to inspect the nearest flower bed.

"Bruno," warned Matthew. "Remember what I said. NO DIGGING!"

Bruno looked surprised, as if such a thought had not even entered his head.

"Honestly," Matthew muttered to himself, "I think I work twice as hard as any of the other Petsitters. If we win that Cup, I should be the one to take it home."

Just then he saw Sam coming toward him and hoped she hadn't overheard.

But she obviously hadn't because she waved and called out, "Hello, Matthew. I thought I'd find you here."

"Hello, Sam," he said. "How are you getting along with Oscar?"

"We've got a bit of a problem," she said. "That's why I wanted to see you. My dad won't let me keep Oscar in the house."

"I thought you said he wouldn't mind."

"He doesn't usually, but it turns out he's got one of those things about rats. What do you call it—a phobia? Anyway, he can't stand them, so he's made me put Oscar out in the garden shed."

"Oh, that's all right then," said Matthew, relieved.

"No, it's not. He says it's only until I can make other arrangements. So I was wondering . . . "

"No," said Matthew firmly. "Sorry, but I've got enough to do walking Bruno."

Sam looked disappointed. "In that case I'll have to ask Jo."

"Good idea," said Matthew. "It's about time he did a petsitting job."

"I'll go and find him now."

When Sam had gone Matthew whistled to Bruno, but Bruno took no notice. He was far too busy digging a hole in a municipal flower bed.

Matthew groaned and raced toward him. "Bruno, stop that!" he commanded.

But Bruno couldn't even hear him. By now he had dug so far down that his ears were buried. Only his hind legs showed above the surface. And of course his tail, which was wagging furiously.

At that moment the park keeper appeared. "It's that dog again!" he spluttered. "Get him out of my flower bed this instant!"

"Yes, sir. Right away, sir." Matthew tried to grab Bruno's tail, but it was wagging so hard it was like trying to catch a windmill.

The park keeper shook his fist. "I warned you last time, if you can't keep him under control . . ."

At last Matthew managed to get a grip on Bruno's hind legs. He gave them a tug and Bruno came shooting out of the hole like a cork from a bottle. Taken by surprise, Matthew fell back onto a clump of begonias, flattening them into the ground.

"All right, that settles it!" The park keeper glared down at both boy and dog.

25

"From now on you're banned—and if I catch you in my park again I'll report you to your principal. Oh, yes! I've no doubt Mr. Grantham would be very interested to hear what one of his pupils has been getting into!"

Matthew struggled to his feet, very red in the face. If the park keeper reported him to Mr. Grantham they'd probably lose half the points they'd already earned! He put Bruno on the leash and hurried out of the park.

✳ ✳ ✳

Mrs. Wimpole was old and bent and walked with a cane, which was why she couldn't take Bruno out herself. "People say I shouldn't keep a dog," she told Matthew. "But it's for the company, you see. I suffer something cruel with my arthritis. If it weren't for Bruno, my life wouldn't be worth living."

She loved Bruno. He could do no wrong in her eyes. So when Matthew told her what Bruno had done in the park, she just laughed.

"Little rascal!" she said, patting Bruno's head. "He's always loved digging holes. By nature he's a hunting dog, you see. In olden times he'd have made a good ratter."

"A ratter? You mean he'd have chased rats?"

"Of course he would." Mrs Wimpole chuckled. "First sniff of a rat and he'd be off like an arrow from a bow."

Which was another good reason, thought Matthew, for not offering to look after Oscar. Not with a ratter living next door. That would be asking for trouble.

He wondered how Sam was getting along with Jovan . . . .

Chapter 3

Phobia

"Sorry," said Jovan, "but your dad's not the only one to have a phobia about rats. I can't stand them either, and I'm sure my mom feels the same."

"But—" began Sam.

"It was rats that spread the plague in the Middle Ages, you know." Jovan shuddered.

Sam tried again. "But—"

"Killed millions of people. The Black Death, they called it."

Sam gave up. She could see it was no use protesting that Oscar was a fancy rat, not a wild one. Or that he was a friendly little animal, very clean and tidy in his habits. In the short time he had been living in the garden shed, she had grown quite fond of him. If only people didn't have this stupid phobia.

"Oh, all right," she said with a sigh. "I'll have to tell Alice we can't look after Oscar."

Jovan looked a bit ashamed. "My mom knows Alice's mother. They're very good friends. Perhaps she could persuade Mrs. Hope to let Alice keep Oscar at home?"

Sam shook her head. "If your mom

feels the same as you do about rats she'd only make Mrs. Hope even more determined to get rid of him."

She felt awful as she walked home, especially when she passed the supermarket and saw where their ad was posted. The ad said

ANY PET LOOKED AFTER
LARGE OR SMALL
WE ARE THE EXPERTS!

But that wasn't true. They couldn't look after fancy rats.

She found her father working in his den.

"It's very odd," he said, looking at her over the top of his drawing board. "Up to this morning I could have sworn I had only one daughter. Now all of a sudden I have two."

"What do you mean!" she asked.

He held up the cartoon he was working on. It showed a small girl with bangs at the kitchen sink, filling a bowl with water.

"Alice Hope," said Dad. "She seems to have moved in with us—hadn't you noticed?"

"She comes to see Oscar," said Sam.

"So I gathered. She's spending all her time in our shed, except when she comes indoors to get water for Oscar. Or lemonade for herself. Or a hard-boiled egg from the fridge."

"Oscar likes hard-boiled eggs," said Sam. "I cooked some for him this morning."

"Mmm." Dad turned the page of his sketch pad over—and there was a huge rat, greedily gulping down a hard-boiled egg.

"That doesn't look a bit like Oscar," said Sam. "Dad, if you'd only get to know him better, I'm sure you'd like him. He's really a very nice little rat."

Dad shook his head. "In my vocabulary the words 'nice' and 'rat' do not go together. Sorry, but you'll have to find another foster home for him."

Heavy-hearted, Sam went out to the garden shed.

Alice sat on the floor, holding Oscar and talking to him quietly as she fed him little bits of hard-boiled egg. As soon as she saw Sam she stopped talking and looked up nervously.

"Hello, Alice," said Sam. "Dad says you've been here all day."

Alice nodded.

"Won't your mother be wondering where you are?"

Alice shook her head.

Sam drew a deep breath. "I'm afraid Dad won't let me keep Oscar here much longer. He doesn't like rats, you see. He's got a phobia about them."

Alice stared at Sam, holding her breath.

"The trouble is," Sam went on, "a lot of people seem to have phobias about rats. Jovan won't have Oscar either, and Matthew says he's too busy. So . . . can you think of anyone else who could look after him for you?"

Tears came into Alice's eyes. Her mouth began to tremble.

Sam said hastily, "Why don't you ask your teacher at school tomorrow? She may know of somebody. Or one of the other kids might offer to look after him."

Alice's tears splashed onto Oscar's back.

"You'd better put him in his cage now," said Sam. "It's time you went home."

Reluctantly Alice put Oscar back in his cage. She stood staring at him as if unable to drag herself away.

"He'll be quite safe," Sam assured her. "Dad always locks the shed at night."

Alice hesitated, then turned and ran out of the door.

Sam felt awful. Poor Alice. There seemed no solution to her problem. She stared down at the cage. Oscar was really rather a timid little rat, quite different from the dangerous monster everyone imagined him to be. He stood up on his hind legs, woffling his whiskers, as if appealing to her for help.

"Don't worry," Sam told him. "I'll think of something, I promise."

That night she lay awake for hours. Surely there must be *some*one who wouldn't mind looking after Oscar! She must find a solution to the problem by tomorrow.

But when tomorrow came and she went out to the shed to check on Oscar, she found she had an even bigger problem.

The cage was empty!

Chapter 4

Rats!

At breakfast next morning Jovan made a startling discovery.

His mother did not feel the same as he did about rats.

Amazing!

And yet perhaps not so amazing when he stopped to think about it. His mother was crazy about all kinds of wildlife. She watched every single nature program on TV. She put food out for squirrels and would never kill a spider, even when it fell in the bathtub. So when she said that rats were enchanting little creatures and badly misunderstood, Jovan shouldn't have been so surprised. But he was.

"Oh, nonsense!" she said when he reminded her about the Black Death.

"That was mainly caused by us humans leaving our garbage lying around. Anyway, you can't blame one small tame white rat for something that happened hundreds of years ago. No, Mrs. Hope is wrong not to let Alice keep Oscar at home and I will tell her so. Leave it to me!"

Jovan couldn't wait to tell the others. As soon as he got to school he spotted Matthew and Sam talking in the playground and rushed over to them.

"Hey, listen," he began without stopping for breath. "My mom's going to persuade Mrs. Hope to let Alice keep Oscar. That means we won't have to worry about him anymore."

But Matthew and Sam did not look pleased. In fact they looked downright miserable.

"Oscar's gone," said Sam.

"Gone?" Jovan stared at her. "Gone where?"

"I wish I knew. He's disappeared into thin air."

"Was the cage door open?" asked Matthew.

"Yes, but the shed was still locked. I know because I had to get the key to open it."

"Then Oscar must still be somewhere in the shed," said Jovan. "It stands to reason."

43

Sam sighed. "I've searched everywhere. Behind the mower. Under the shelves. Inside the garbage bags. There's no sign of him."

"He must have found a hole and got out," said Matthew. "I bet he's hiding in your garden."

"That's where I was looking when Dad called out it was time to leave for school," said Sam. "I didn't dare tell him what had happened. He'd go bananas if he thought there was a rat running loose in our garden."

"Have you told Alice yet?" asked Jovan.

"No." Sam lowered her voice. "Luckily she didn't come by this morning before school. But she's bound to come by later this afternoon. I thought maybe I'd go home at lunchtime and search again."

"We'll come with you," said Jovan,

"What about Katie!" asked Matthew. "Do you think we should tell her?"

"Better not," said Sam. "You know what little kids are like. She'll only go and tell Alice, and then Alice will start crying and—"

45

"Okay, okay," said Matthew quickly. "I won't say a word."

They agreed to meet as soon as morning school was over and go straight to Sam's house.

But at lunchtime Jovan and Sam were waiting by the school gates when Katie came running up.

"Matthew gave me a message," she told them. "He said you're not to wait for him but to go ahead. He'll catch up with you later." And then, in the same breath, "Where are you going?"

"Home," said Sam.

"Why?"

"Because—because my dad's ill and I want to make sure he's okay," said Sam.

"But why are Jovan and Matthew going with you?"

"Because—because—oh, I haven't got time to explain. Come on, Jo."

They hurried off before Katie could ask any more questions. "I think we should have told her," said Jovan. "She's pretty quick for a little kid. She'll soon figure out that something's gone wrong."

"It's Matthew's fault for giving her the message," said Sam. "What do you think he's doing?"

Her question was answered when Matthew met them outside her house with a small black and white dog.

"I went to ask Mrs. Wimpole if I could borrow Bruno," he said. "He's a ratter, you see. If Oscar's around he'll find him much quicker than we could."

Jovan glanced at Bruno, who was wagging his tail so hard it looked as if it might come off any minute. "What'll he do if he does find him?" he asked warily. "He won't kill him, will he?"

"He might," said Matthew. "But if I keep him on the leash we should be able to stop him in time. As soon as he starts sniffing around, we'll follow him, wherever he goes."

They took Bruno into the shed. When they showed him the cage he got very excited. They let him sniff the wood shavings and he got even more excited.

They showed him some leftover bits of hard-boiled egg and he ate them.

"Now what do we do?" asked Jovan.

They all stared at Bruno and he stared back, wagging his tail.

"Rats, Bruno!" said Matthew encouragingly. "Go find the rats!"

"There's only one rat," Jovan pointed out.

"Doesn't matter," said Matthew. "He'll work harder if he thinks there's more than one. Rats, Bruno. Go find the *rats!*"

Suddenly, Bruno seemed to understand what they wanted. He leaped to his feet and raced to the door, dragging Matthew behind him.

"Come on, he's got the scent!" shouted Sam.

Chapter 5

A Nice Little Snooze

Matthew let himself be dragged first this way, then that. Sam's garden was pretty wild. Bruno had never had such a good time in his life. It was like being in the park, only a hundred times better because he was allowed to go where he pleased.

As soon as he reached the vegetable patch he started digging.

54

"I think he's found something," called Matthew.

Sam and Jovan came rushing up. "What's he found?"

"I don't know yet. But he's wagging his tail like crazy."

They stood watching as Bruno scrabbled away at the hole. The earth piled up behind him as he dug deeper and deeper. At last he stopped digging and started gnawing at something.

"Quick, stop him!" urged Sam. "If that's Oscar . . ."

But it wasn't Oscar. It was a bone. An old bone. A very, very, very old bone. Possibly even a fossil, which at any other time Matthew might have found interesting. But not now. He took the bone away from Bruno and threw it into the bushes.

Bruno tried to chase after it, but Matthew wouldn't let him. "Oh no you don't!" he said sternly. "*Rats*, Bruno—that's what you're supposed to be hunting for. *Rats!*"

It wasn't long before Bruno started off on another scent, dragging the Petsitters behind him. But the scent seemed to lead him around in circles. As they passed the house for the third time, a window flew open and Sam's father stuck his head out.

"I'm trying to work in here," he protested. "Anyway, why aren't you at school?"

"Sorry, Dad," panted Sam. "But—but —Matthew had to walk the dog."

"And this seemed the safest place to do it," said Jovan.

"I wouldn't have thought it would take three of you to walk a dog." Her father

glanced at his watch. "You'd better be quick. School starts again in fifteen minutes."

He closed the window.

"Whew!" said Sam with relief. "He's right, though. There's not much time left. Hurry up, Bruno. Rats, rats!"

But after another five minutes spent chasing around the garden, the Petsitters came to the conclusion that Bruno wasn't much use as a ratter.

"I guess he's out of practice," said Matthew. "I'd better take him home to Mrs. Wimpole."

"Okay, but don't be long." Sam and Jovan hurried off back to school.

Matthew took Bruno straight to Mrs. Wimpole's house and rang the bell. There was no reply.

He rang again. Still no reply.

"Oh, no!" he groaned. "She must be having her snooze."

Every afternoon after lunch Mrs. Wimpole had what she called a "nice little snooze" in the armchair. Matthew went to the window and peered into the living room, but he couldn't see inside because of the net curtains. He knocked on the glass. This time he thought he heard a noise, but it was very faint.

"I bet that's her snoring," he told Bruno. "What am I going to do with you?"

Bruno wagged his tail.

"I could put you in our house for the afternoon, but Mom and Dad are at work and you'd probably howl. Or I could skip school and stay home with you, but I'd only get into trouble." Matthew chewed his lip, trying to decide. At last he said, "No, I'll have to take you with me. It's the only answer."

The first person he met as he hurried into school was Mr. Grantham, the principal. Just his bad luck!

"Hello, Matthew," said Mr. Grantham. "You're late."

"Yes, sir. I'm sorry, sir."

"And what are you doing with that dog? It's not Pet Day, as far as I recall."

Once a year the school had a Pet Day, when everyone was allowed to bring their pets to school. But that wasn't until next semester.

Matthew decided the only thing to do was tell the truth. Well, part of the truth anyway. "It's Mrs. Wimpole's dog, sir. She can't take him out herself because she suffers something cruel from her arthritis, so I walk him for her every day."

"Ah, so this is part of your Petsitting service," said Mr. Grantham with a nod. "Very commendable, but I'm afraid you can't start looking after pets at school. You must take him back."

"I've tried, sir, but I couldn't make her hear. I think she's having her afternoon snooze."

"I see." Mr. Grantham frowned. "Well, you certainly can't take him into class. You'd better put him in my office."

"Yes, sir. Thank you, sir."

"But I'm only helping you out this once, you understand? I don't intend to make a habit of it."

"No, sir." Matthew sped off with Bruno.

He took him into Mr. Grantham's office and unclipped his leash. "Now, Bruno," he said sternly. "You've got to behave yourself in here, do you understand?"

Bruno wagged his tail.

Matthew glanced anxiously around the room. As far as he could see there was nowhere Bruno could possibly dig a hole.

"Lie down," he commanded. "And go to sleep."

Obediently Bruno lay down and put his nose between his paws.

"Good dog. I'll be back for you as soon as school's over."

Matthew closed the door behind him and hurried off to class.

Chapter 6

Weird!

Katie couldn't figure it out.

Why had the other three Petsitters gone off at lunchtime to Sam's house?

Sam had said it was because her father was ill and she wanted to make sure he was okay. But why had Matthew and Jovan gone with her? Something weird was going on, Katie felt sure. Something the

65

others didn't want to tell her. But *why?*

She kept thinking about it all afternoon. The first class was art, which was good in one way because while she was painting she could go on thinking. In another way it wasn't so good because she wasn't exactly brilliant at painting. Not like Alice Hope.

"Today I'd like you to illustrate summer," Mrs. Baxter, their class teacher had said when she handed out the paper.

Summer! How on earth were you supposed to illustrate that?

Katie cast an envious look across the table. Alice's painting was a colorful mass of blues and greens and yellows. Perhaps, if she used the same colors . . .

Then she noticed something odd.

Alice was wearing her winter sweater. In the middle of June. When everyone else was wearing short sleeves or no sleeves, Alice had sleeves right down to her wrists. Weird!

Katie leaned across the table. "Have you got a cold or something?" she asked.

Alice shook her head.

"Then why are you wearing your winter sweater?"

Alice didn't answer. She went on painting.

Weird!

Then Katie noticed something even weirder. A face was poking out of Alice's left sleeve where it rested on the table.

A small face with whiskers. And pink eyes. And a woffly nose . . .

Oscar!

No, it couldn't possibly be Oscar. Oscar was safe in his cage in Sam's garden shed . . . .

Katie leaned across the table again. "Did you know," she whispered to Alice, "that you've got a rat up your sleeve?"

Alice seemed not to hear her. Katie was about to repeat the question when she noticed that the whiskery face had disappeared. Perhaps she had imagined it?

Just then Mrs. Baxter stopped by their table. "Oh, Alice, what a lovely picture! It exactly captures the feeling of summer, all the warmth and light and brightness of the sun. But why are you wearing your winter sweater?"

Alice turned pink. She stared down at her painting.

Katie said quickly, "I think she's got a bit of a cold, Mrs. Baxter."

"Has she? What bad luck. These summer colds are so difficult to shake off." She leaned over Alice's shoulder. "Perhaps you could add a little more green . . . ."

71

At that moment Katie noticed a large bump under Alice's sleeve. A bump moving slowly but steadily up her arm. Now it had nearly reached her shoulder. Any minute now that whiskery face was going to appear out of the neck of Alice's sweater—and if it did Mrs. Baxter would be sure to see it.

Katie thought hard. Somehow she had to draw Mrs. Baxter's attention away from Alice. She glanced at the jar of dirty water not far from her left hand . . .

WHOOSH!

"Oh, Katie!" exclaimed Mrs. Baxter. "Look what you've done—and all over Alice's beautiful picture."

"Sorry, Mrs. Baxter." She looked quickly at Alice and was relieved to see that the bump had moved down her sleeve again.

"There's water all over the floor. You'd better go and get the mop."

"Yes, Mrs. Baxter."

The mop and bucket were kept in the custodian's closet at the other end of the school. As Katie hurried down the corridor she saw Matthew knocking on the door of the principal's office.

"What are you doing?" she asked.

"Mr. Grantham sent for me," he said. "I think I'm in trouble."

"I'm in trouble too," she told him. "I spilled a jar of water all over the floor of our classroom. But I had to do it. You see, Alice Hope—"

Before she could finish, Mr. Grantham opened the door. "Ah, Matthew White," he said in a very stern voice indeed. "And Katie, too. You'd better both come in."

"Why me?" said Katie quickly. "I haven't done anything. Well, I did spill a jar of water, but that wasn't—"

"You're a Petsitter, aren't you?" Mr. Grantham opened his door a little wider. "Then you may as well see what one of your pets has done to my office."

Katie peered inside. No doubt about it, Mr. Grantham's office was in a terrible mess. The wastepaper basket lay on its side, and there were bits of chewed-up paper strewn all over the floor. And in the middle of the mess, wagging his tail, sat a small black and white dog.

"Bruno!" Katie exclaimed. "What's he doing here?"

"Your brother brought him to school," said Mr. Grantham. "And I foolishly said he could stay in my office. What Matthew failed to tell me was that this was a seriously delinquent dog."

"He's not really delinquent," said Matthew, looking embarrassed. "But he does like digging holes. He must have tried to dig one in your wastepaper basket."

"Which confirms my suspicions that—apart from on Pet Day—animals in school are not a good idea," said Mr. Grantham. "You must take this dog back to its owner right away."

"What—now, sir?"

"Yes, now. And if she's still sleeping you must wake her up." He handed Matthew the leash. "Go on."

Katie watched with amazement as Matthew clipped the leash to Bruno's collar and hurried off. Mr. Grantham hardly ever let anyone go early, at least not unless they were ill. She wondered what Matthew was doing with Bruno at this time of day anyway! And what did Mr. Grantham mean about Mrs. Wimpole being asleep?

Weirder and weirder . . .

"All right, Katie, you can go," said Mr. Grantham.

She hurried off to the closet. *Animals in school are not a good idea*, he had said. She wondered what he would say if he knew that Alice Hope had a rat up her sweater!

Chapter 7

Petsitters For Ever!

Matthew rang Mrs. Wimpole's bell twice and rattled the doorknob. Nothing happened.

"She must be sleeping very heavily," he said to Bruno.

Bruno put his head on one side and whined.

"Sssh!" said Matthew. "I think I heard

her snoring . . . ."

He bent down to peer through the mail slot. To his surprise he saw Mrs. Wimpole lying on the carpet in the hall, which seemed a very odd place to take her afternoon snooze. But she wasn't snoring, she was moaning. And her legs were all askew, as if she had fallen down the stairs . . . .

"Mrs. Wimpole!" Matthew called through the mail slot. "Mrs. Wimpole, are you hurt?"

She tried to raise her head. "Matthew! Oh, Matthew, I'm so glad you've come. I—can't get up . . . ."

"I'll get the police," said Matthew. "My dad's on duty. He'll know what to do."

The first thing Matthew's dad did was call an ambulance. Then he came rushing up in a police car with the siren blaring and forced open the front door.

Soon Mrs. Wimpole was carried out on a stretcher. When she caught sight of Matthew she asked anxiously, "Where's Bruno?"

"I've put him in my house," said Matthew. "Don't worry, we'll look after him."

She tried to smile. "Thank you," she whispered.

Matthew's dad told him later that Mrs. Wimpole had broken two ribs and her collarbone. But she was now resting comfortably and was expected to make a good recovery.

Later that day Matthew and Katie went to Sam's house.

"My dad says I may have saved Mrs. Wimpole's life," Matthew told the other Petsitters proudly. "He said if I hadn't turned up when I did she could have gone on lying there for hours and hours."

"And all because you borrowed Bruno!" said Sam.

"And because Bruno wrecked Mr. Grantham's office and got sent home," said Katie.

"It just goes to show that walking old ladies' dogs *is* a worthwhile job," said Jovan. "Even if it does get a bit boring at times."

"That's what my dad said." Matthew looked even prouder. "He thinks I might get my photo in the paper. He thinks the Petsitters may even become famous!"

The others cheered. "Petsitters are brilliant!" said Sam, giving the two thumbs-up sign. "Petsitters forever!"

But then she added, "Well, not all that brilliant. Remember why we borrowed Bruno in the first place?"

"To try and find Oscar," said Matthew with a sigh.

"The worst part is that my mom's persuaded Mrs. Hope to change her mind," said Jovan. "She says Mrs. Hope's prepared to give Oscar a second chance."

"So Alice could have taken him home," Sam said gloomily. "If only we hadn't lost him."

Katie looked puzzled. "What do you mean, you've lost him?"

"Sam found his cage empty this morning," said Matthew. "We didn't tell you before. We were afraid you might tell Alice."

"Well, you should've," said Katie indignantly. "Because I could have told *you* that Oscar isn't lost. Alice's got him. She's been hiding him under her sweater all day."

The other Petsitters stared at her.

"I don't believe it!" said Sam.

"She must have sneaked back yesterday evening before you locked the shed," said Matthew. "But why didn't she take the cage as well?"

"Hiding a rat under your sweater's hard enough," Katie pointed out. "Trying to hide a cage would be even worse."

"That's true," Sam agreed.

There was a knock on the front door. Sam went to answer it.

She came back with a much more cheerful-looking Alice, holding Oscar in her arms.

"She's come for his cage," said Sam. "I told her how worried we've been about him and how naughty she was to take him without telling us."

Two tears appeared in Alice's eyes.

Jovan said hastily, "Has your mom told you that you can keep Oscar at home?"

Alice nodded. The tears disappeared.

At that moment Sam's father came out of his den. "I heard the doorbell. Who—?" He stopped as he caught sight of the small white creature in Alice's arms. "Oh, no! Not the rat again."

Alice clutched Oscar tightly, as if to protect him.

Cautiously Dad took a closer look.

"I have to say, he is a nice little fellow. Reminds me of a tame mouse I used to have when I was a boy." He patted Oscar's head and went back into his den.

"Well, honestly!" exclaimed Sam. "All this trouble we've had because people have a phobia about rats. And then, when they meet one, all they can say is 'What a nice little fellow'!"

Oscar sat up in Alice's arms and wrinkled his nose.

"You know what I think?" said Matthew. "I think it doesn't matter about winning the Cup, because being a Petsitter is brilliant anyway. So whatever happens next Friday I think we should continue petsitting."

The others agreed. And when Friday came and the Community Service Cup went to the group who had been visiting the elderly, the Petsitters didn't mind a bit. They gave each other the two thumbs-up sign and silently cheered:

PETSITTERS ARE BRILLIANT!
PETSITTERS FOREVER!

The End

Join the Petsitters Club for more animal adventure!

1. Jilly the Kid
2. The Cat Burglar
3. Donkey Rescue
4. Snake Alarm!
5. Scruncher Goes Walkabout
6. Trixie and the Cyber Pet

Look out for:

8. Where's Iggy?
9. Pony Trouble

Petsitters Summer Special: Monkey Puzzle